Grandpa Lou,
What Can You Do?

Written by Willie Etta Wright
Illustrated by Anwargart

Dedication

I dedicate this book to biological grandparents and to all who assume the role of a grandparent. Your love, support, and sacrifice enhance the lives of your grandchildren.
This book is dedicated to every grandfather who diligently embraces the title of being a Girl Granddad.
I also dedicate this book to all senior citizens who continue to exercise their creativity and ageless potential.

I live with Grandpa Lou and Grandma Mae
Because my mommy has gone away.
I'd ask, "Will she ever come back for me?"
Grandma would say, "She will, Bella Marie!"
Sometimes I really felt lonely and sad,
But living with them wasn't that bad.
Grandpa's and Grandma's hugs made me smile.
They made me feel happy for a while.

When I'm not playing with my friend, Kaye
I loved being close to Grandma Mae.
She tried to find things for me to do.
But I'd whine, "I'm bored," when I was through.
Grandma sighed, "Bella, I have to keep you busy.
If not, I'll feel like I'm getting dizzy."
She made up a song about me.
It was called, "Bella, the Busy Bee."
I loved when she said, "Come help me cook."
Sometimes she told me to read a book.

One day she said, "I'm getting ready to go.
I have to see about Aunt Flo."
I begged, "I'll be good. May I go too?"
She said, "No, Grandpa will take care of you."
When you're bored find things to keep busy.
You don't want to make your grandpa dizzy.
She hugged us and said," Good-bye."
When she left I just had to cry.

Without Grandma I felt all alone.
"Grandpa," I asked, "may I use your phone?"
Nobody answered the phone but Kaye.
I asked, "Could you come over to play?"
She said " I can't. I'm going on a trip."
We're going on a big cruise ship."
I said, "Wow, you're like leaving me too!"
Now sadly I had nothing to do.
I gently rubbed Cuddles' soft, warm fur.
I guess I had to just play with her.

I rolled out of bed the next day.
I thought, "I'm going to be bored today.
Why couldn't I have fun like Kaye?"
Now I really missed Grandma Mae.
I searched for something good to eat.
Did Grandma forget to leave a treat?
A bowl of cold cereal would do.
I didn't want to bother Grandpa Lou.

Each day after Grandma went away
Grandpa asked, "What's up for me today?"
One day I asked, "Could we like bike ride?"
He grunted, "I can't. I hurt my side.
My back aches, and my knees feel sore.
Ride your bike. I'll ride my lawn mower."

Pedaling was so hard in the heat.
Grandpa said, " Let's stop for a treat."
We stopped at Frosty's Ice Cream Shop.
I was so happy to finally stop.
He bought me a cup and a cone.
I ate while he talked on the phone.

The next day I asked, "How about Splash Park?"
He said, " No, soon it'll be dark
Besides I can't see well at night.
We should have gone when there's sunlight.
Find your bathing suit and come outside.
Your playset will be your waterslide."
I couldn't believe the fun that I had.
Staying with Grandpa wasn't so bad.

One day I asked, "Could we like play basketball?"
Grandpa said, "I can't jump at all.
I'll teach you an easy way to play.
Sit down, aim, and toss the ball that way."
I didn't miss the wastebasket a lot.
But Grandpa Lou didn't miss a single shot.
The Wastebasket Ball Toss was kind of fun.
At least Grandpa didn't have to run.

One day I said, "Let's have a tea party, Grandpa Lou.
I'll wear a tutu. Will you too?"
He said, "I can't wear something like that,
But I'll see how I look in that hat."
Grandpa told stories while we sipped tea.
This was like the best party to me.

One day Grandpa announced, "Someone's here!"
The TV was so loud that I couldn't hear.
He gently tapped me on my head.
"Bella, look who's here to see you," he said.

I wondered to myself, "Who could it be?
Maybe someone was here to play with me."
I turned around to see the surprise.
Was I dreaming? I rubbed my eyes.
"Mommy!" I screamed. "I really missed you!"
She cried, "Bella Marie, I missed you too!"
Mommy and I hugged, kissed, and cried.
I couldn't stop screaming. I really tried.
"Mommy," I begged, "Please stay with me!"
She replied, "It'll be soon. You'll see."

Grandpa hugged me as I yelled, "Yes!"
He chuckled, "I knew what to do. I guess."
I said, "You did! I had fun with you.
You're like the best ever, Grandpa Lou."

THE END